USBORNE FIRS[T]
Level [I]

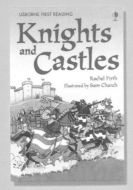

Usborne First Reading
Knights and Castles
Rachel Firth
Illustrated by Sam Church

Usborne First Reading
The Golden Carpet
Retold by Mary Masenna
Illustrated by Débora Marcero

Usborne First Reading
RUNAWAY PANCAKE
retold by Mairi Mackinnon
Illustrated by Silvia Provantini

Usborne First Reading
Percy and the Pirates
Russell Punter
Illustrated by Kate Sheppard

An Aesop's Fable
The Hare and the Tortoise
Retold by Susanna Davidson
Illustrated by John Joven

Usborne First Reading
The Goose Girl
Retold by Russell Punter
Illustrated by Qin Leng

Usborne First Reading
Sleeping Beauty
Retold by Lesley Sims
Illustrated by Sara Gianassi

Usborne First Reading
The Elves and the Shoemaker
Retold by Rob Lloyd Jones
Illustrated by John Joven

Usborne First Reading
Jack and the Beanstalk
Retold by Susanna Davidson
Illustrated by Lorena Alvarez

How Tortoise Tricked the Birds

Retold by Clifford Samuel
Illustrated by Giusi Capizzi

Reading consultant: Alison Kelly

Late one afternoon, a storyteller sat outside.

I have a story to tell you.

Children gathered around her under the shady trees.

Once, long, long ago, *everyone* was hungry.

There was no rain, so there were no plants to eat.

Tummies rumbled. All the animals dreamed of food.

The sky gods looked down
at the hot, dry earth and the
hungry creatures.

"How can we help?"
they wondered.

"Let's invite the birds to a feast! They can fly to us."

Down came the invitation.
The birds were very excited.

They painted their bodies
with beautiful patterns.

I want to look
my best for
the Sky Feast!

They danced and they sang.

But they were being
watched... by Tortoise!

In those days, Tortoise had
a smooth, shiny shell.

He was also cunning and greedy and *very* hungry.

His eyes lit up when he heard about the feast in the sky.

He hadn't eaten for weeks.
His body rattled in his shell
like a pebble in a pail.

"I must get to the Sky Feast.
But how?" thought Tortoise.
He began to plot and plan.

"No," said the birds. "We don't trust you. You're always full of tricks."

"Not any longer," said Tortoise. "I've changed."

Tortoise had a trusting
tongue. All the birds
believed him.

"But you can't fly,"
said a cuckoo.

"Aha!" replied Tortoise.
"But I *could*. I just need a
feather from each of you."

18

And so the birds each gave
Tortoise one of their feathers.

Now you can fly with us to the feast.

When it was time to leave,
Tortoise called to the birds.

"Before we go," he said, "we must each take a new name. That is the rule of Sky Feasts."

All the birds nodded. "Tortoise is so wise!" they thought, believing him.

"I will take the name *All of You*," said Tortoise.

Then they set off, swirling through the sky.

The birds flew gracefully.
Tortoise flapped awkwardly.

They were all a blur
of bright feathers. Up, up, up
they went...

At last they arrived.
Tortoise greeted the sky gods.
He gave a long speech.

He spoke very well. The birds were delighted that Tortoise had joined them.

Thank you for inviting us...

Out came the food... the most tempting dishes Tortoise had ever seen.

The stew came hot from the fire in a big pot.

There was coconut rice. *Mmm!*
Okra soup. *Yum!* Breadfruit
porridge and yams...

It smells
delicious!

"Who is this food for?"
asked Tortoise.

"It is for all of you,"
replied the sky gods.

Tortoise looked at the birds with a sly smile. "That is *my* name, remember?"

That means this food is MINE! ALL MINE!

And Tortoise began to
eat. The birds watched.
They were furious!

Tortoise guzzled
and gobbled...

...until he was nearly
bursting out of his shell.

The birds took one angry look at the empty plates and decided to fly home.

But first, they took back *all* of their feathers.

Now Tortoise had no wings to fly home.

He only had his hard shell and his full tummy.

"Please," he begged the birds, "will you take a message to my wife?"

Parrot gave a sigh.

What's your message?

"Tell my wife to lay out all the soft things from inside our house," said Tortoise.

"Then I can jump down and land safely."

But Parrot had other ideas.

Parrot told Tortoise's wife
to lay out all the *hard* things
she could find.

Tortoise's wife brought out
rocks and pots, shovels
and hoes.

Tortoise looked down from the sky. He could see the pile was ready...

...he just couldn't see *what* was in it.

Tortoise shut his eyes.
"One... two... three... JUMP!"
he cried.

Down fell Tortoise. Further
and further, faster and faster.

"Will this fall ever end?"
he wondered. And then...

CRASH!

Tortoise lay very still
on the floor.

His shell was SMASHED
to pieces.

His wife ran straight for
the doctor.

Oh, my
poor
husband!

The doctor stuck Tortoise's
shell back together. It took
a *long* time.

"So you see," said the storyteller, "that is why Tortoise has a shell like a jigsaw!"

*In memory of my mother: a huge thank you for teaching
me about West African stories and life, and for being my
friend. Your support meant the world to me. With love.
– Clifford Samuel*

About the story

How Tortoise Tricked the Birds is a story from
the Igbo people of Nigeria. Similar stories
also appear in *Aesop's Fables* and Indian myths.

About the author

Clifford Samuel is an award nominated actor,
and writer. He's of Nigerian heritage and has
strong Igbo roots.

Edited by Susanna Davidson
Designed by Jodie Smith
Series designer: Russell Punter
Series editor: Lesley Sims

First published in 2022 by Usborne Publishing Ltd., Usborne House,
83-85 Saffron Hill, London EC1N 8RT, England. usborne.com

USBORNE FIRST READING
Level Four

USBORNE FIRST READING

The Story of
Pinocchio

Retold by Andy Prentice
Illustrated by Jesus Lopez

USBORNE FIRST READING

Clever Jack
and the Giants

Retold by Susanna Davidson
Illustrated by Lee Wearley

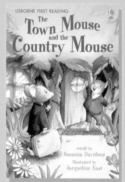

USBORNE FIRST READING

The
Town Mouse
and the
Country Mouse

retold by
Susanna Davidson
Illustrated by
Jacqueline East

USBORNE FIRST READING

Dick
Whittington

London
10 miles

Retold by
Russell Punter
Illustrated by
Barbara Vagnozzi

USBORNE FIRST READING

The Story of
Baby Jesus

Retold by Mary Kelly
Illustrated by John Joven

USBORNE FIRST READING

The
Reluctant
Dragon

Based on the story by Kenneth Grahame
Illustrated by Fred Blunt

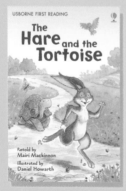

USBORNE FIRST READING

The
Hare and the
Tortoise

Retold by
Mairi Mackinnon
Illustrated by
Daniel Howarth

USBORNE FIRST READING

Goldilocks
and the
Three Bears

Retold by
Susanna Davidson
Illustrated by Mike Gordon

USBORNE FIRST READING

Thumbelina

Retold by
Susanna Davidson
Illustrated by Petra Brown